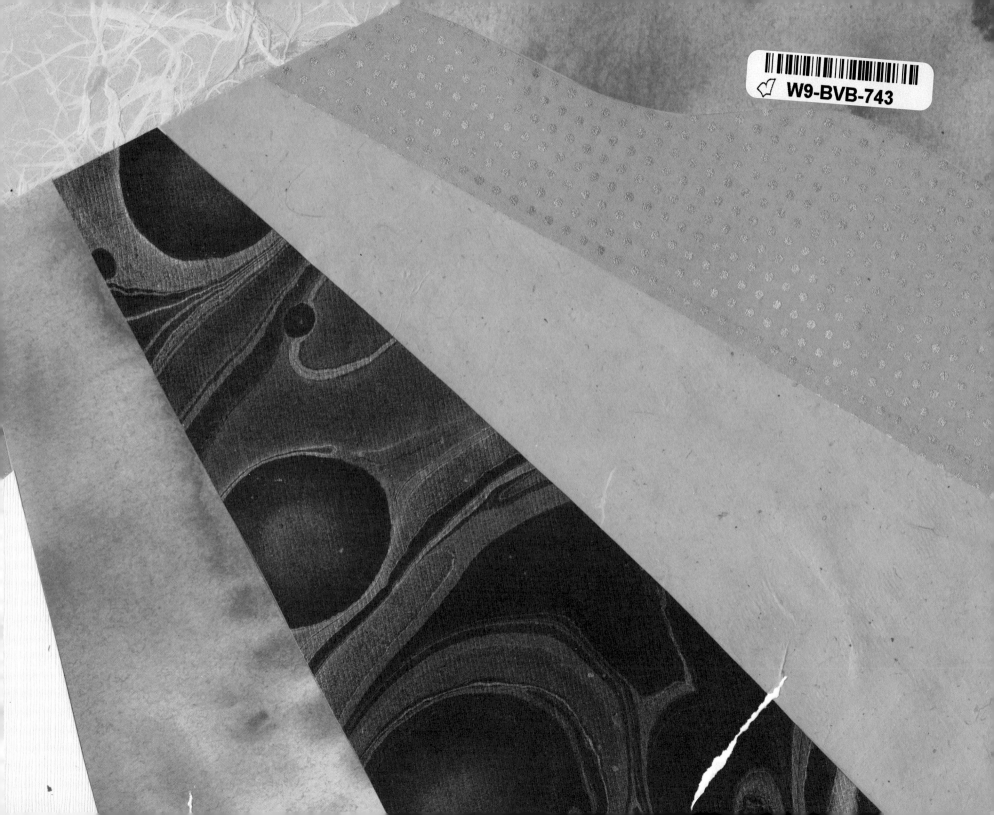

PLAYTIME
for Restless
RASCALS

words by **Nikki Grimes**

pictures by **Elizabeth Zunon**

sourcebooks
jabberwocky

For Coda Bates, an expert at play from Day #1!
—NG

For Chauncy.
—EZ

Text © 2022 by Nikki Grimes
Illustrations © 2022 by Elizabeth Zunon
Cover and internal design © 2022 by Sourcebooks

Sourcebooks and the colophon are registered trademarks of Sourcebooks.

The full color art was created using oil and acrylic paint with cut paper collage, marker, and gel pen.

Published by Sourcebooks Jabberwocky, an imprint of Sourcebooks Kids
P.O. Box 4410, Naperville, Illinois 60567–4410
(630) 961-3900
sourcebookskids.com

Cataloging-in-Publication Data is on file with the Library of Congress.

Source of Production: Wing King Tong Paper Products Co. Ltd., Shenzhen, Guangdong Province, China.
Date of Production: April 2022
Run Number: 5025239

Printed and bound in China.
WKT 10 9 8 7 6 5 4 3 2 1

"Time to get to **WORK**, little one," I tell you.

"WHAT WORK?" you ask.
Like always,
you pretend not to understand.
"Your job is called

PLAY,"

I say.

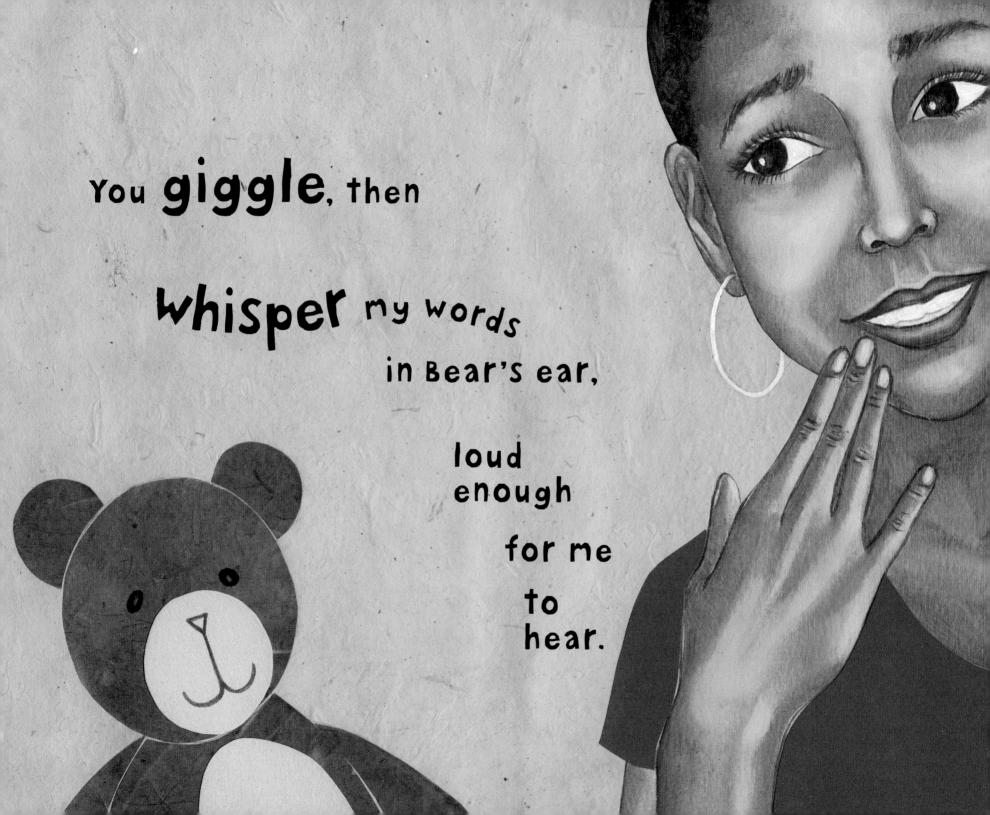

You **giggle**, then **whisper** my words in Bear's ear,

loud
enough
for me
to
hear.

"Bear says that's not a real job," you tell me.

"Is that so?" You nod your head so hard, your curls bounce.

But Bear and I both know, when it comes to PLAY,

you're an expert.

on rainy days,
you dance in puddles
and paint your legs

with mud.

on sunny days,
with a little help from me,
you rock the backyard swing
near enough the sky
to tiptoe

across the
sun.

In the fall,
you dive into a mound
of **orange**, *gold*, and
fire-red leaves,

then toss them into
the air and yell

"**CATCH!**"

But the sky
never plays the game,
SO YOU
WiN!

In winter,
you and your shadow
track through fresh snow,
leaving just one pair
of footprints.

All by yourself,
you make a row
of **angels,**

then mold the best snowwoman
I've ever seen, and give her

MiTTENS

so her hands
won't get too cold.

You'd play all day,
if I let you.
But halfway through,
I call, "Time for lunch!"

"No!"
you say,

But I sweep you up in my arms, and shush you with a KiSS.

After lunch,
I do the dishes

while
you
pour
make-believe
TEA

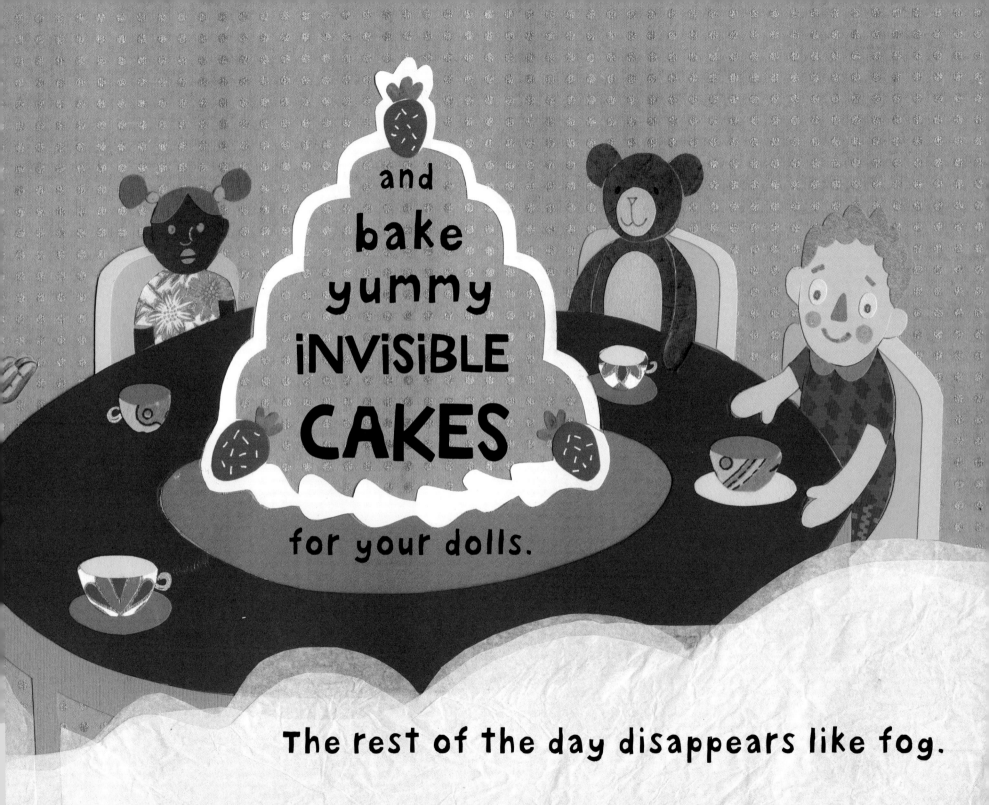

and bake yummy INVISIBLE CAKES for your dolls.

The rest of the day disappears like fog.

sometimes you build

TRAINS and TRUCKS,

and ride them on far

away adventures.

sometimes you race your toy cars along the smooth track of your window sill.

out front, you jump rope, or cartwheel across the lawn, landing a perfect

TEN!

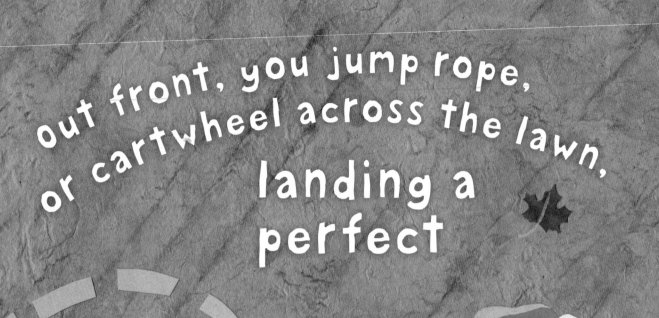

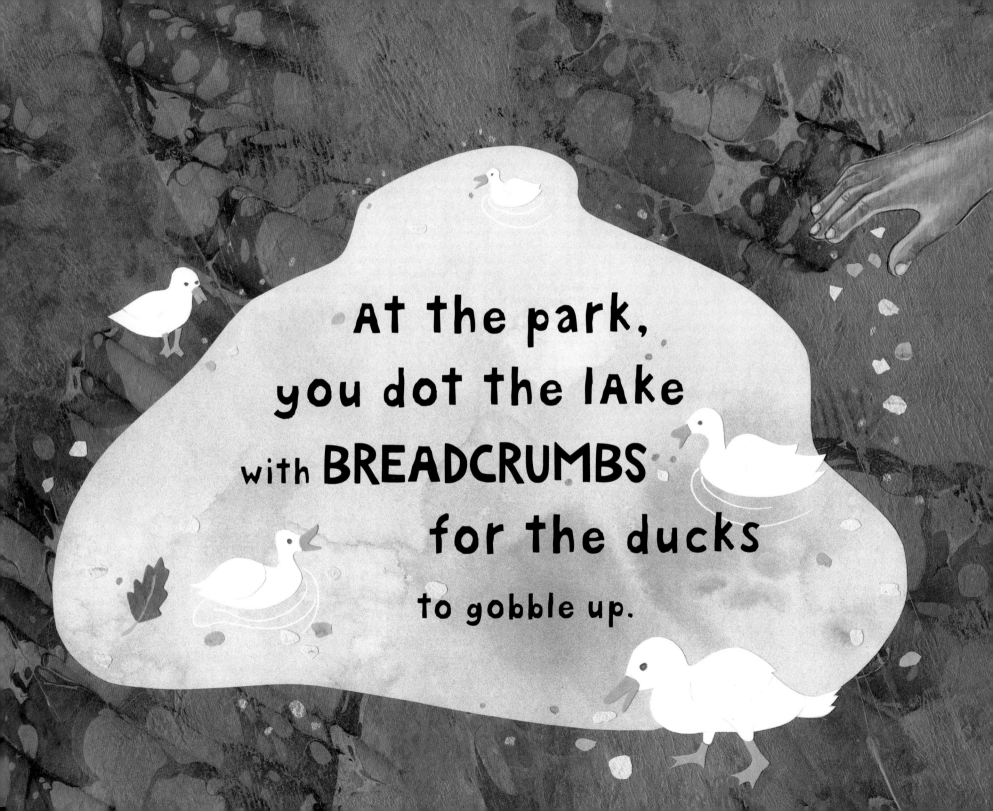

At the park,
you dot the lake
with **BREADCRUMBS**
for the ducks
to gobble up.

Sometimes you careen around the world on the **WOODEN CAROUSEL** and never want to get off.

The minute you do, you say, **"MOMMY, MOMMY, MOMMY!** Let's go again!"

Most of all,

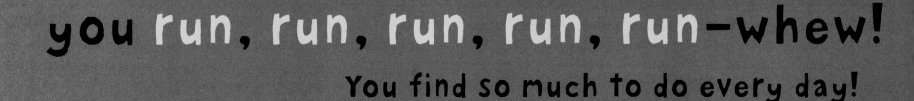

you run, run, run, run, run—whew!

You find so much to do every day!

Sometimes, in late afternoon, you drag out a

PUZZLE

or board game.

"Puleeeeeze!"

you say,

but your poor mama is

BEAT.

I drop to the sofa
and pull you up onto my lap
so we can both cuddle and nap.

"Let's be still
for a few minutes,"
I say.

And we fall asleep...

...until we hear the front door open.

"DADDY, DADDY, DADDY!"

You scramble off my knee

and run into your father's arms.

"**whoa!**" he says.
"Let me get in the door!"
You pretend patience for two seconds,
then pull out a board game and plead,

"**DADDY,**
DADDY,
come play!"

"Your turn," I say, when he looks in my direction.

The next thing I know,
the two of you are on the floor.
I curl up on the sofa

and close my **eyes** once more.

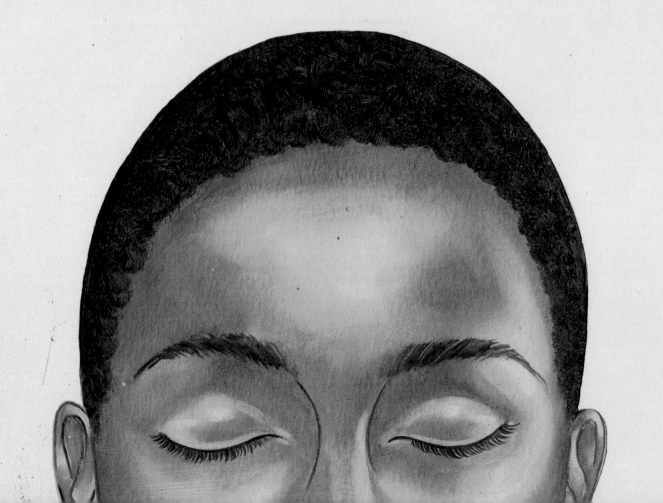

and your daddy and I both know,

you're an expert.

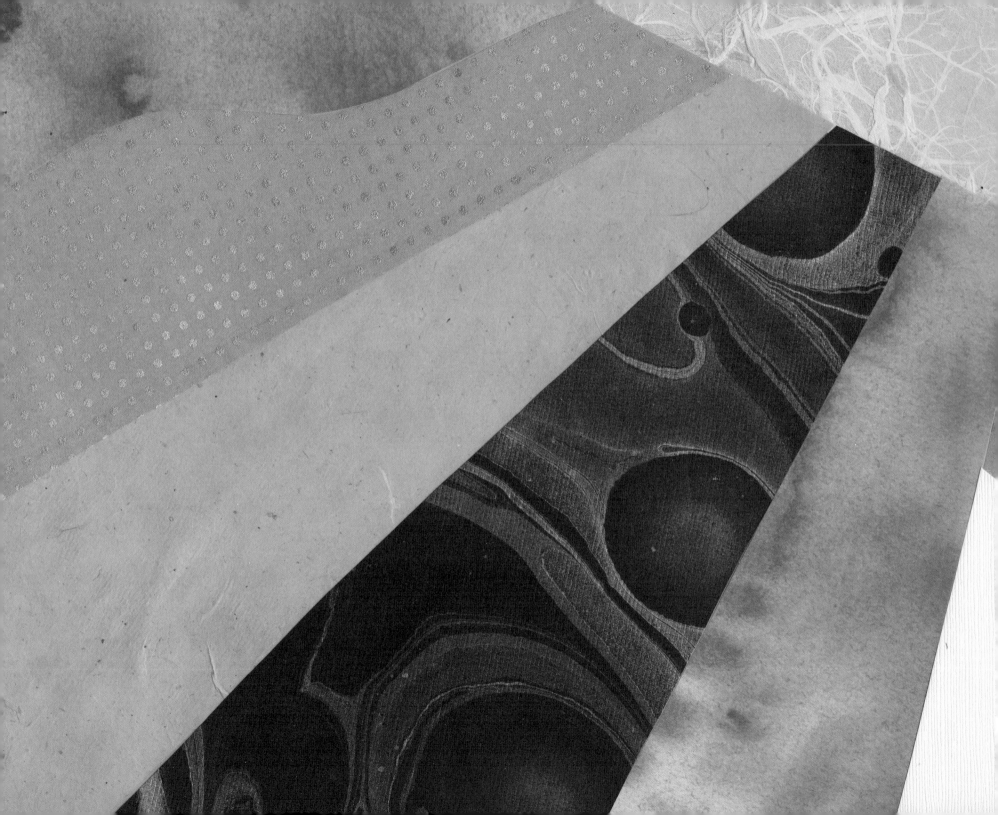